# THE SCENE FROM THE BUS

To Pat,
The best helper!
Love,
Carol Tankersley
2017

# THE SCENE FROM THE BUS

Xulon Press
2301 Lucien Way #415
Maitland, FL 32751
407.339.4217
www.xulonpress.com

Printed in the United States of America.

ISBN-13: 9781545617243

"THANKS"
To my husband Tony,
for his love and encouragement,
and
for pushing me to get this book published,
and
for his understanding of my need,
at 2 o'clock in the morning,
to dash to the computer,
and
to my grandsons Joseph, Jacob and Isaac,
of which one or all three, who asked,
" You like giraffes, when are you getting one?"
and
to Tony's great-granddaughter, Ava,
who named the giraffe,
and
to his granddaughter, Audrey,
who expressed an interest,
to teach in Africa,
and
to all my family and friends
for their interest,
and
LOVE.

# Chapter 1

The view from the bus was beautiful. The blue sky, the vegetation with its several shades of green and the colorfully painted native huts all added to the calliope of color.

The ride so far had been extremely bumpy due to the sun baked uneven dirt roads. The bus was an antique, to say the least. It had evidently been repaired and rebuilt many times with scraps and cast offs from several different vehicles making it appear somewhat strange looking.

Suddenly out of the corner of Lisa's eye a scene appeared and then in the blink of an eye, it was gone. She quickly closed her eyes, trying to make her mind bring back the scene that had been so vivid for that split second in time. Something about that image made her very uneasy.

Then there it was just as she remembered it. A tall tree in full green foliage and a very tall, tawny spotted giraffe munching on its leaves. But the strangest part of the scene was what was sitting on the ground close to the giraffe's long legs. A beautiful baby camel. The baby camel's long eyelashes gave the appearance of it being half asleep and its body language radiated a sense of sadness.

The picture then faded away and once again left Lisa with an even more uneasy feeling. Her thoughts soon turned to the events leading up to her decision to come to Africa. Lisa's Mom had passed away when Lisa was in her senior year of college. She left school and became her Mom's main caretaker. After her Mom passed away Lisa returned to finish school, graduated and was soon teaching at an elementary school near her home.

Two years ago, her Dad suddenly became ill and passed away. His health had always been good and his passing was totally unexpected. Last year she applied for and was granted a position at the mission school. She sold the house, with everything in it, and moved to Africa. So far, she had not regretted that decision for a moment.

The bus continued riding on its way and Lisa soon arrived at the school. She stiffly rose from her seat and descended the bus's rickety steps. The school holiday was almost over. Arrangements had been made for her to pick up the school supplies sent from the Mission Board. Bags and boxes were soon placed on the ground, at her feet, by the driver and then tipping his cap, he waved goodbye. The bus was once again on its bumpy way.

The school's caretakers, Miriam and Martha, quickly appeared to help their favorite and only teacher. The twins knew that somewhere in those packages would be a treat for them. Something specifically chosen by Lisa and then, requested to be sent along with the school supplies. They would patiently wait because they knew their treat would eventually come.

With their help, everything was neatly put away in a few minutes. Silently, the caretakers, M and M, left her rooms. Lisa had given them the nicknames M and M because of the brilliant colored ribbons they wore tucked into their short hair. The ribbon's colors reminded Lisa of her favorite M and M candies.

The heat of the day and the bus ride finally took its toll and she plopped down on her bed. Sleep came almost instantly. She woke up with a start and felt as if she had been asleep for only a few minutes. It was then that she realized it had been the scene with the giraffe and baby camel which had awakened her and with it came that feeling of unease, again.

Sleep, much less rest, was now out of the question. Lisa had to do something. But what? She now had a quest and in some way, something would be resolved. Lisa had slept longer than she realized because night had fallen. Her stomach now reminded her that she had not eaten since breakfast.

She quickly prepared and just as quickly ate her dinner. Cooking was not one of her interests. Clothes and shoes for the next day were placed on the chair next to her closet. She put the bus schedule, snacks and money in her handbag on the chair. Next, she took her shower, brushed her teeth and then jumped into bed. Pictures and questions were soon swirling in her mind. "I can't do anything tonight," she said to herself and, if as on a signal, sleep finally came.

# Chapter 2

$\mathcal{T}$he early morning sunlight coming in through Lisa's window awakened her. She jumped up from her bed and became a whirling dervish. First, washing her face and then brushing her teeth. Next, she was putting on her clothes that had been so carefully laid out on the chair the night before. Lisa was, during all this time, drinking from a cold, water bottle and eating a piece of bread with cheese. Shoes were put on last and grabbing her handbag, she was out the door.

The worn and tattered printed bus schedule indicated that the bus arrival time was to be between 8 and 9 o'clock. In reality, arrival time could really be anytime between 8 and 10 o'clock. Never early and most times late due to the weather, the roads, the roaming animals, mechanical problems and/or anything else imaginable that could interfere with the printed schedule arrival time.

Lisa waited at the so-called bus stop, which was only an unmarked area under a tree closest to the road. A dust cloud appeared in the distance. It was now 8:30 and Lisa crossed her fingers and said out loud, "Oh, let it be the bus coming!" Sure enough, twenty minutes later the bus arrived and Lisa climbed aboard. She was on her way.

"On the way to where?" was the question that kept bugging her. That split-second image gave no indication of the village's name. Lisa would have to rely on her instincts to find it. The bus jostled on through the first town and this morning for some reason the ride seemed to have more bumps then yesterday morning.

It was as if a lightbulb went off in her head." What if I use the printed scheduled bus stops and combine that information with the time spent riding between villages. Then with my arrival time at the school, maybe I can find the village. Wow, this is a big help".

Her face lit up after only a few calculations. The result, if true, was that the village she wanted would only be two villages away, and it was.

There again was the tall, tawny giraffe standing by that same tree eating leaves or its' cud or whatever. Lisa quickly left the bus, shook her head and took a double take. She realized that the baby camel was not there. Lisa kept looking around for the camel as she cautiously walked toward the giraffe. For some reason she thought of that old saying," Music calms the savage beasts" and she started softly humming.

"I never realized how majestic and elegant giraffes are," she was thinking as she walked to within 2 feet of the giraffe. Then a soft voice from somewhere behind her said, *"Missy, be careful to not make sudden moves or she will run off."*

Lisa kept humming as she slowly turned around. There stood a small, thin native man grinning at her.

"Do you know anything about the giraffe? Like why does he stay here in this spot? Does anyone look after him?" Her questions came gushing from her mouth like a waterfall with the words tumbling over each other. *"Missy, firstly the giraffe is lady giraffe. See long black hairs coming from tuffs on top of head. Men giraffes no have long hair on tufts. Nextly, she be lonely lady and stay by our village for company and I tink she like this tree's leaves."* Lisa was full of questions. The natives, once meeting you or hearing good things about you, would always have time to answer questions or just talk. Most of the local villagers had taken advantage of English language classes at the Mission or many of their children attended school there. In one way or another the village kept up to date with what was happening at the school.

Suddenly remembering her manners, Lisa said, "Oh, I am so rude. My name is Lisa Grant and I teach at the Mission school and your name, sir?"

The man's whole demeanor changed. He stood taller, but again grinning from ear-to-ear, and said, *"Yes, Missy I know who you are. I had only one year at the school but they graduate me anyway from your school long time before you come here. My name is Judah. We learned much from Bible and I took name because Judah was warrior."*

"Judah, where is the baby camel?", Lisa asked anxiously.

*"Don't know, Missy. She girl baby camel. She come and go looking for food, I tink. The tree is too*

*tall for her to reach leaves. Lady giraffe throw some leaves on ground but not enough for growing baby."*

Lisa's eyes began to tear. " Oh, Judah we have to find her. She is so tiny and defenseless." By this time, Lisa was extremely upset and asked, "Is there someone I can talk to about this? Like a government agent or tribal chief and where can I find them?"

Judah quietly answered, *"Go to tall white building at end of village. Ask for John."*

Lisa thanked him, shook his hand and headed off to the tall white building.

By now the morning sun had risen high in the sky and the heat index seemed even higher. Lisa was sweating, not perspiring or glistening, but sweating. Just as she reached a door to the building the door opened and a deep voice said, "I saw you coming. Welcome and who might you be?"

The glare from the sun caused her to squint and that screwed up her entire face. What a sight she was standing there sweating and squinting. Then after entering the air-conditioned building, the cold air hit her like a wind chill in Chicago. When the man saw her start to shiver it must have scared him and he became concerned.

"Are you OK?" he asked anxiously.

"Yes, sir. This coolness was a shock but it feels wonderful. I just cannot get used to this heat, as you can see by my perspiring. Oh, I am sorry, I am forgetting my manners again and that makes it twice today. I am Lisa Grant from the Mission School and I am looking for someone called John."

Laughingly, he said, "Well, Lisa Grant I am John. John Purcell, Resident Agent. I have only seen you from a distance since you arrived. So, hello and welcome to Africa. Now let's get you something to drink and then we can see if I can help you?" He gestured to a room with a table, chairs and a small refrigerator. Bottled water and glasses soon appeared and they both sat down at the table. Lisa took a sip and proceeded to explain her quest. Every detail of the scene that had made her feel so uneasy was described precisely. She sounded and spoke just like the teacher she was! All the while she was talking, John's eyes never left her face. He was listening intently and taking in every word and his mind was registering every detail and nuance about her.

# Chapter 3

*L*isa finished her tale, sat back in her chair and finished drinking her water. "Is there a restroom I could use. It has been a long morning and I would like to freshen up."

"Of course, come right this way and take your time. I am going to see about some lunch for us. Is that all right with you?

"Absolutely all right and that would be great. Thank you so very much."

The light lunch was perfect. Cold fruit, chicken salad, warm rolls and iced tea. Lisa hoped that he would not notice how hungry she had been by how quickly she had eaten. Someone else's cooking always tasted so much better to her then her limited cooking skills.

John suggested that they move to the screen enclosed porch. The porch overlooked the preserve. It had ceiling fans and what looked like comfortable chairs. The hot afternoon sun caused everything, animal or human, to appear to be moving in slow motion.

"What exactly do you do here, John," Lisa asked quizzically.

"This sanctuary preserve has many purposes. The WILDLIFE and RESEARCH projects take care of the orphaned or injured wild life. The Bushmen Clinic provides accessible affordable primary healthcare for the under privileged Bushmen community.

"But what do you **do**?", Lisa asked again.

In a stern voice with a heavy accent he replied, **"If I tell you, I will then have to kill you."**

He smiled and added, "But you know about the under privileged Bushmen because your mission school helps with their education."

Suddenly his whole demeaner changed and when he spoke it was with a quiet anger.

"The Bushmen have lived on this land for tens of thousands of years. They know the land and how nature has a hand in providing a living. But in 1980 diamonds were discovered on their land and the government forced the Bushmen out. Their homes and water supply was destroyed. Their schools and health clinics were closed. Imagine, the government came not once but on three separate occasions. They made sure that the area was purged from anything that would show the Bushmen's contribution to maintaining a way of life and their connection to the land. Thank goodness, this preserve was built some distance away from the mines and the Bushmen living here in the preserve can get medical help. Oh, I didn't mean to get on my soapbox. To answer your question, my job is to maintain the hospital buildings, manage the preserve's labor force and I just help wherever I can. Just do what has to be done."

A quietness came over the room. John's mind was spinning with thoughts of the injustices. Lisa sat quietly because of everything she had just heard. To her, this was a lot to absorb at one time.

"I understand your frustration about the Bushmen. My reason for coming here was to help the mission in whatever way I could. I didn't know a lot of what you just told me about the Bushmen. It was so unfair. Such gentle and knowledgeable people. I have learned a lot from my students but not about what happened in the past. I need to learn more."

Lisa then said in a haughty voice, "After all, I can have a soapbox too."

This seemed to lighten the mood in the room and John asked, "OK. Now what is really bugging you?"

Lisa looked at him, cocked her head to one side and said," The baby camel was not with the giraffe."

John said," Did I hear you correctly the first time and again now that this is about a giraffe and a runaway camel?"

Rising from her chair, with her blue eyes blazing and growing larger and larger, she raised her five-foot-two body as tall as possible and said in a staccato voice, "She is a baby camel. Not a big camel! She is so little and defenseless. We need to find her. **Now**."

"OK. OK. We need to start with Judah. From what you said he is the one who knows the most about these animals." All the while he was talking, he was thinking to himself," Boy, if I were a kid in her class, I wouldn't want to get on her bad side!"

They were soon riding in John's air-conditioned truck on their way to the other end of the village and Lisa thought to herself, "Judah doesn't have anything else to tell. I asked the right questions. Ha!"

Too soon the ride was over and there was the giraffe but no baby camel. John parked quite a distance from the giraffe and they quietly exited the truck. Slowly walking towards the giraffe, John recognized the tag attached to the giraffe's ear. It was Ava. John had been called out to check on Ava more times than he could count and now he wondered if there was such a thing as a delinquent giraffe?

Lisa had instinctively begun humming and John looked at her in alarm. She slowly raised her finger to her lips indicating for him to be quiet. When they were close to the giraffe, a soft voice behind them said, *"Missy Lisa you do well."*

Not having heard anyone approach them, John and Lisa both slowly turned around and all the while Lisa kept humming.

Judah indicated for the three of them to move further away from the giraffe and they did.

*"So-o-o good to see you, John, sir."* Judah said with his usual grin. *"And you too, Missy Lisa."*

Before John could say anything, Lisa said, "Oh, Judah I found John right where you said he would be. Thank you so much. We have come to ask for your help."

*"Don't know what more help I can give. I give you everting I knowed about baby camel,"* Judah answered.

Thinking to herself, Lisa thoughts were, "See I was right. Judah told me everyting he knowed. I mean everything he knew."

"OK, Ranger John. What do you suggest we do next?", Lisa asked in her most condescending voice. Ignoring her addressing him as Ranger John, he, in his most business-like voice asked, "Judah, when was the last time you saw the camel? I mean the baby camel."

*"Two or three days back now I tink. What is meaning of ranger?'*, Judah said quickly and quizzically.

Just as quickly John spoke up and said, "Judah, Missy Lisa tried to make a joke. Just call me John, please and thank you. Now, is there anyone in the village who would take in and care for an animal? A youngster or older person looking for company?"

*"Hollie Smokie! I tink I knowed who it could be. Momma With Big-Toe. She have no children. No family. Lonely Momma. Come. I show you her hut,"* he answered excitedly.

# Chapter 4

*J*udah quickly started walking and Lisa was right behind him. Their quickness caught John off guard and he hurried to catch up.

The hut appeared to be smaller than the other huts. If Momma With Big-toe lived alone that could be the reason why. The ground in front of the hut was neat and clean. It showed signs of having been recently swept, probably with tree branches. Peering around the back of the hut they saw a small structure and there next to it was the tethered baby camel.

Lisa could not constrain herself. "Oh! Oh, my! See, there is the baby camel." Lisa was ready to run to the camel when John grabbed her arm and held her back.

"Lisa, first we need to speak with Momma. We need to be conscious of her feelings. Let's go see her," John said quietly in her ear.

All three approached the bright fabric door flap and Judah softly said, *"Hello, Momma With Big-Toe. Speak with you please?"*

A wizened face with a wide toothless grin and wearing a brightly colored turbaned head-dress appeared suddenly through the hut's folded-back fabric door flap. *"Judah, you come see Momma? Good, good. Too long time you no come."* and out the door she came in a matching brightly colored dress. Surprise showed on her face when she spotted Lisa and John.

*"Judah, you no say utters wid you,"* Momma's words to him were like a reprimand.

*"Hello, Missy from school. I know about you. You good teacher. And hello to you, John, sir. We move to tree over there. Too hot in my hut,"* and she proceeded to gently push them along to the benches under the tree. As soon as everyone was seated, Judah spoke first. *"Momma we need help about baby camel. She so little. She need to have doctor take care of her. OK if we take her to preserve hospital?"*

Momma's toothless grin disappeared and suddenly she looked so old and sad. *"Baby keep me company and give much pleasure. Judah. John. Missy, but we do what best for baby. Yes?"*

John softly said," Yes, Momma that is best. The baby camel is not from this area and maybe needs special care. Besides, I want to find out how and why the baby is here. When you want to see the baby camel, I will take you to the preserve. Then if you wish, you can have your toe checked out at the Bushmen Clinic."

Momma's face broke out in a grin once again. *"You take me in your truck to see baby camel and maybe my toe? Oh, Judah you bring good friends. I call you friends? Yes?"*

Relief flooded Lisa's face. John watched Lisa intently as she tried not to cry while answering Momma.

"Yes, Momma we are friends. Thank you for letting us take the baby camel to the hospital" having said that, they all stood up and headed toward the back of the hut.

The baby camel looked in good health. Whatever Momma had been feeding her seemed to have been fine. As they approached and then were close, Momma spoke soothingly to the camel and recognizing Momma's voice, the baby responded with little noises. The baby camel was soon untied and Lisa placed her arms around the baby camel's neck nuzzling her and humming the entire time.

Then Lisa stood up and standing as tall as possible, looked at John and said "Please, place the baby camel right behind your front seat and I will sit in the back next to her." John, recognizing that stance knew Lisa would not have it any other way.

"Goodbyes" were said and Lisa and John went on their way. Not a word was spoken between them until they reached the preserve. John was the first to speak, "I'll drive right to the animal hospital to see if Doc is around."

Lisa was still quiet. He didn't sense that she was sad, maybe just relieved to have found the baby camel. He hoped that someday she would tell him why it was so important for her to find the baby camel. He realized that he would just have to wait till then.

## Chapter 5

John drove his truck close to the front of the hospital and just then a figure came walking out of the main door. It was Doc. John parked the truck and opened his door.

"Well, John. We don't usually see you this time of day. It's almost dinner time! So, what's up?", Doc asked.

John was just about to answer him when Doc spotted Lisa and the baby camel. "Well, knock me over with a tree branch! Who be those two good-looking creatures riding with you, John?" asked Doc.

"Doc, this is Lisa Grant a teacher at the school and that is a female baby camel, "John answered with a wide grin.

"I know what a camel looks like, Doc answered. But where did it come from? And as to the lovely female grown up teacher lady, I recognize her from around the school. Let's go inside and get out of this heat."

"By the way Doc, this baby camel was hanging around with that delinquent giraffe, Ava. Judah seems to think they were both lonely and keeping each other company," John said with a wink of his eye.

"That could be. Animals have a keen sense of assessing another animals' needs or what we call feelings," Doc answered in his professional voice.

The hospital foyer was delightfully cool but as they approached the work area the air began to get warmer. "We can't keep the animals too cool, 'cause that is not what they are used to. I will be in the exam room that has a small room next to it with a glass window. Lisa, you can stay behind the glass window and watch while I examine the baby camel."

Lisa did as Doc suggested but John stayed with Doc. The baby camel was no feather weight and was soon hoisted up in the air by straps and other mechanical means. Then it was lowered slowly on to an antiseptically cleaned stainless-steel examining table. First, the baby camel was laid on its right side and its left side was checked. Then, it was turned over and its right side was checked. Next, it was laid on its back for a tummy check. During all the time it was being poked and prodded by Doc's skillful hands, Lisa noticed Doc's mouth moving. Maybe Doc was softly talking to the baby because John, from what she could tell, spoke not at all.

From Lisa's perspective the worst came next. Its small ears and throat were examined with tiny cold looking metal instruments. And just when Lisa thought it was over, a thermometer was placed in the baby's rear. Lisa was beside herself. She looked like a parent watching her baby being examined for the first time. Thankfully Doc knew what he was doing and the exam was quickly over.

Not being able to hear what was being said, Lisa opened the room's door as fast as she could and went into the examining room.

"This female baby camel is in pretty good health for not having a mother to care for her," Doc said in his most professional manner. John tried hard to keep from laughing because that was not the low-key, unobtrusive individual speaking that everyone had come to know and love.

"The medical staff will come up with a formula and or food and a feeding schedule for her. Now I'll go and find a place for her to stay while she is in quarantine."

QUARENTINE! What do you mean, Quarantine?" Lisa asked in a panicky voice.

Doc answered with his deep calming voice," Lisa, all animals brought to us have to be quarantined for a short time. This allows us to make sure that the new animal is safe to be around our other animals. That includes humans, too"

"But Doc, she has been around other animals and humans already. She is so little to be suddenly put somewhere all by herself. Can't an exception be made for her?", Lisa, almost in tears, quickly asked.

"Come with me. I will show you that she will not be alone and how we will make her comfortable." Doc said soothingly.

As the two of them, completely forgetting that John was in the room, were about to leave the exam room, John said," I know what happens next and because I have something I want to check on, Doc, can you take care of the girls till I get back?"

"Sure. We three will be busy for a while and then we humans can have dinner. OK by you John? Doc said smiling.

"Maisie's cooking always sounds good to me," John said hoping his mouth would not start to drool.

John's mind had been elsewhere during the previous conversation. He had suddenly remembered hearing or reading something about a poaching band of natives that were caught somewhere north of the preserve. His thought was to talk with the area's police outpost as fast he could. His two-way radio was in his truck and to the driveway he went.

Doc took Lisa to the animal hospital part of the complex. It was a large part of a huge building. Long hallways, long enough that roller blades could be great fun. They passed four rooms of offices with desks and chairs when they suddenly arrived at a wall completely made of see through glass inside the room were small cubicles with glass doors. All of them appeared empty.

Doc opened the hallway door to the hospital room and Lisa walked through with Doc following her. Three staff members, in their medical garb, were busy at whatever they were in the process of doing. Hearing Doc's voice they stopped and turning from their stations saw Doc holding the baby camel.

"Wow, she is tiny", came from one staff member. "What is a dromedary camel doing way down here?" came from another. The third staff member just walked over to Doc and without a word, took the baby camel from him and started humming. Lisa was taken back by what seemed to her to be approval for her instinct to hum when near the giraffe and again with the baby camel.

Doc introduced Lisa to Larry and then to Joe, who was also called Moe and next to Jane, who was called Curley. Lisa could not help but laugh when hearing their names. Doc explained that he was very fond of the old THREE STOOGES movies and watched them over and over. Now, Jane had gorgeous red, curly hair and her nick name made sense. But as to Joe being called Moe, Lisa guessed one would have to spend time there to figure that out. "What a dedicated and fun group they appear to be," she thought to herself. Suddenly Lisa sensed a change in the room's dynamics.

Doc asked, in a fake Southern drawl," OK, you 'all, is everything ready?" to which Larry answered "Yes, sir. Blankets, alarm clock and fresh cut grass are waiting over there."

Joe, with his genuine Southern drawl, was next and answered, "Yes, sir. Weight, age and metabolism charts are ready for you."

Last to speak was Jane. She was still humming softly while holding the baby camel when she answered, "Yes, sir. I made calls around to the bordering areas to no avail There has not been any reports of a female camel showing up anywhere."

"Thanks. You'all have done great in such short notice. Now let's show Lisa how we will take care of the baby. This is ridiculous. This baby camel needs a name. Come on Lisa. You seem to be her guardian. Speak up," and Doc said.

In a flash, Lisa was taken back to her childhood. The hair stood up on the back of her neck and taking a deep breath, she answered, "Um, how about Cutie Pie or does that sound too strange?"

Everyone in the room seemed to sense that this was an important moment for Lisa. There was more importance to this name than she appeared to give it. Almost in unison and almost at the same time, the trio replied with, "Oh, perfect" or "Sounds fine to me" or "She is a cutie pie. Look at those eye lashes". Doc laughed and said, "OK. OK! Her name shall forever be Cutie Pie. Now, let's show Lisa how we will take care of Cutie Pie.'

Lisa for some reason was deeply moved and had a hard time paying attention to what was being said. She saw the blankets and freshly cut grass placed inside one of the cubicles. Then the alarm clock was wrapped up in another blanket. This too was placed in the cubicle.

"Lisa. Lisa." Lisa heard someone saying her name and quickly shook her head as if to clear her mind. "Yes, I'm sorry. I must have zoned out. It has been a long day. I can see that Cutie Pie will be in good hands, thanks to all of you."

Jane said softly, "Don't worry, there is always one of us on duty. Someone will be here to talk to or to hold or to play with Cutie Pie. She won't be alone."

"Jane, thank you for letting me know all of that and I have a question? Lisa said.

"Fire away", Doc replied.

"What is the alarm clock used for?" was Lisa's answer.

The room echoed with their laughter and Larry answered, "We get that question all the time. The alarm bell part is removed and when the clock is wound all that remains is the ticking sound. The ticking sound is, well, like a heartbeat to the animal and helps to keep them calm. They also seem to sleep better."

Cutie Pie was placed in a cubicle and after a few minutes, she fell asleep.

"You think of everything", Lisa was saying just as John knocked on the glass window. Everyone followed Doc out the door and crowded around John.

## Chapter 6

"*I* spoke with the police outpost about the baby camel and I have news."

"OK, John don't keep us in suspense. Out with it," Doc said.

"A band of poachers from up north had stolen some animals and one of them was the orphaned baby camel. The police were following the poachers whose escape route was not far from Judah's village. With them when they were finally caught, was a young boy. During questioning by the police, the boy asked if anyone knew of a baby camel. It seems that he had been afraid that during their running from the police, something would happen to it. So, late one night as they were passing by Judah's village, he quietly took the camel and left it by the tree. He hoped someone would take care of it. Lisa, that must have been right before you saw them together."

Lisa with tears in her eyes replied, "Oh, what a kind thing for that boy to do. I hope the police are not too hard on him!"

"Evidently he is an orphan himself. The police are trying to find any relatives that would take him. He just went with the poachers because they let him help with the animals and gave him food and shelter in return. He had been on his own for just a few months. The sergeant I spoke with, really liked the boy and said, "He has good manners and is very respectful. Probation would really be possible if someone would agree to the terms and help him."

"Well, the school could be of some help. John, we need to do something for him. He was so kind to Cutie Pie."

"He was kind to who? And who is Cutie Pie?", John asked quizzically.

Doc laughed so hard that he shook the glass windows. "Lisa has decided that the baby camel is to be called, Cutie Pie. I thought that it was time to give it a name. So, I have decreed that from this day forward, the baby camel shall be forever known to all as CUTIE PIE. So sayeth, ME!"

"OK.OK. What is so funny?" said a voice from the doorway and that started them laughing all over again. Doc, wiping the tears from his eyes, said "Maisie come over here and meet Lisa. Lisa asked John to help her find Cutie Pie and all of us just put Cutie Pie to sleep."

Maisie looked as if Doc had just spoken to her in a foreign language. "What did you just say? Who is Cutie Pie and why did it take all of you to put Cutie Pie to sleep and to sleep where?"

Once again Doc, the staff, Lisa and John started laughing. "Maisie, let's go and eat. We'll tell you everything as we eat. All right with everyone?"

Their reply was unanimous. "Let's go. What are we waiting for?' Everyone scrambled for the door. Jane grabbed a monitor and winked at Lisa. "I'm on duty tonight and I will be watching Cutie Pie while I eat. Don't worry."

Maisie and Doc's home was not far from the hospital building. Its large kitchen served as a kind of commissary for the staff. There was no grocery store nearby. The dining room was used as an eating area for staff and, sometimes, quests. Maisie prepared and cooked the breakfast and dinner meals.

The night's meal proved to be delicious and the evening was fun filled with laughter and lots of jokes. Maisie's questions had been answered. It seemed that she laughed just as hard as the rest of them had when Doc had answered the same questions asked by John. Then, just when it seemed that everyone had finished eating, Lisa learned the meaning of Joe's nick name, Moe.

Joe, looking at Maisie, quietly said, "Mo', please!" which made everyone start laughing all over again. Maisie, while still laughing, explained to Lisa that when Joe first came, he would always ask for more but it sounded like Moe, and that was why Doc came up with the nick names.

When everyone finished laughing, John groaned and said, "Maisie my dear, you out did yourself with this delicious dinner. If I ate like this every night, I would have to widen my doorways and get larger clothes."

Just then, Doc noticed that Lisa was almost asleep while sitting upright with her head against the back of the dining room chair.

"John", Doc said softly, all the while pointing his head towards Lisa, which of course caught everyone's attention." I think Lisa is asleep. It has been a long day for her and it is too far to take her back to the school tonight. Maisie, do we have a guest room ready?

"Always, Doc," Maisie quickly replied. "Come along John I will show you the way."

John, gently and slowly picked up Lisa, so as not to awaken her. This was his first opportunity to get a closer look at her face. Her eyes were closed but he remembered how blue they were. Now he noticed her long eyelashes lying on her cheek. His mind was racing with questions. "Where are you from? What is the real reason you are here? Why are you so concerned about the baby camel? Oops, I mean Cutie Pie."

Maisie said softly, "John, here we are. I'll take over now. Just place Lisa on the bed and go and have some dessert and coffee. Call the school to let them know that she is staying overnight with Doc and I."

"OK, Maisie, sounds great and thanks", John said as he left the room and headed back to the dining room.

# Chapter 7

The next morning, Lisa, not wanting to open her eyes, woke up slowly. Suddenly she sensed that she was not in her own room much less in her own bed! Her eyes flew open as she began looking around the room in every direction for something familiar.

Flashbacks of the previous night's dinner and the ensuing conversations played in her mind. She then noticed she was wearing hospital scrubs and that her clothes were neatly folded on a chair by the open bathroom door.

"Oh, this is Maisie and Doc's home", she concluded with relief. She got up and upon entering the bathroom, saw towels and toiletries that had been placed neatly on a washstand. "They really thought of everything," Lisa said out loud to herself before she gratefully took a shower.

She later dressed, straightened the bed and bathroom, and opened the door to the hallway. Delicious aromas came floating in the air and she let her nose guide her to the kitchen. Maisie was flipping pancakes and browning sausages. She had earplugs in her ears and was loudly singing to a song only she could hear.

Upon seeing Lisa, Maisie did not miss a beat of the song but pointed with her pancake turner, for Lisa to go into the dining room.

Lisa smiled and said loudly," Good morning. Smells Good", but all the while knowing Maisie could not have possibly heard a word of what she had just said.

Jane and Joe were seated at the table eating. Both said, almost in unison, "Good morning. Like the music and the show?" and they both proceeded to laugh and gesture toward Maisie. Jane looked at Lisa and said," Maisie claims that to sing is to pray twice and she needs all the prayers she can get." Seriously, she is the happiest person I know bar none. Lisa, now sit down and eat"

Lisa quickly sat down and began heaping pancakes and sausages on her plate. As she started to eat, she kept staring at Jane. Jane got the message. "OK. Here's the report on Cutie Pie's night. I only have one thing to say and that is, Cutie Pie is a perfect baby. She woke up one time, rolled over and went right back to sleep."

Jane had been watching Lisa and said," Slow down. You are eating too fast. Cutie Pie is fine. When you are finished eating, we'll take you to see her." Lisa's body finally relaxed and she stopped wolfing down her food.

Lisa, red faced and embarrassed by having been told that she was eating too fast, answered Jane and said, "That would be great and thanks!"

The trio soon cleaned off the table and took their dishes to the kitchen. Maisie was still singing loudly while cutting up vegetables for dinner. They waved good-bye to Maisie and shouted their "Thanks."

The morning sun was about a quarter of the way up in the sky and seemed to just hang there above the horizon. A hint of coolness was still left in the air from the night before. Lisa said out loud, "Oh, to me this is the perfect time of day," and both Jane and Joe shook their heads in agreement.

They were almost to the hospital when they saw John's truck approaching. Joe used hand signals to indicate to him that they were all heading to the hospital. John waved and pointed a "thumbs up" indicating that he understood. Lisa meanwhile had continued walking, seemingly even faster, and was the first through the door.

"Hi, Lisa," You need to put on a gown today 'cause all the tests have been done and we await Doc's results." Larry knew better than to elaborate on what tests were taken and what instruments were used. He had heard about her reaction to Cutie Pie's initial exam.

After almost tripping over the gown, Lisa was at the cubicle's glass door in a flash. Cutie Pie was standing at the door peering out and it almost looked as if the camel was smiling.

"Oh, you have really been well taken care of by these wonderful people," Lisa said and then turned to Larry and asked, "When will she be released from Quarantine?" Larry laughed and replied, "You make it sound like she is in prison. When Doc comes by in a few minutes, he will tell us when her sentence is over" and he started laughing all over again.

Just then, Jane, Joe and John came through the door, put on gowns and walked over to see Cutie Pie.

35

Jane looking at Lisa said, "See, I told you that she was fine." Sheepishly, Lisa said softly, "Thanks."

Just then Doc came through the door and upon seeing John, exclaimed, "We haven't had this much excitement and company in so few days since I can't remember when!" Then looking at the others, he announced in a loud voice, "OK. Cutie Pie has passed her tests with flying colors and is hereby set free, so sayeth me."

As soon as he said "FREE", Lisa opened the cubicle door and kneeling, hugged Cutie Pie. The two of them together made a cute picture. It was a true Kodak photographic moment.

# Chapter 8

"John what brings you here so early? Doc asked. "Well, I saw Doc Williams to make an appointment for Momma With Big-Toe and he can see her later today. I just wanted to see you about Momma maybe seeing the baby camel today, too." As soon as the words were out of his mouth, he avoided looking in Lisa's direction and corrected himself." I mean Cutie Pie."

"Momma can come by anytime to see her in here or in the fenced area out back. The yard has a gate that Momma can open." Doc replied.

John quickly went onto some other news. "I saw Judah as I was leaving Momma's. He's amazing. Not only is he very knowledgeable about everything to do with nature but he loves to share his knowledge." John smiled as he continued speaking." Judah looked like a Pied Piper because there must have been every young boy and even some girls from his village following him. Whenever school is not in session he has a kind of nature school. Today I saw his school in action. They were all carrying fishing poles that they must have made for themselves. Some were quite unique I must say. He has the patience of Job, to handle all those kids! When I first arrived here, Judah took me under his wing. I learned more from him in three months then I could have with years of study. He had been working for the preserve since the planning stage and then the beginning phase. Coupled with that and his knowledge about nature, he was an invaluable asset for me. But then his wife became gravely ill. Doc, wasn't she sick for about two months and most of that time she spent here in the preserve's Bushman Clinic?"

"Yes," Doc answered and then continued, "It was such a sad case. Doc Williams and his staff tried everything but to no avail. Everyone there and here, tried to help with her care but Judah would not hear of it. He stopped working and stayed by her side every day and night, acting as her personal nurse."

The staff knew some of Judah's story but not all of it. Lisa knew next to nothing. So, they were all totally captivated by what was being said.

John, in a somber reflecting gaze, looked at Doc and said," I remember when Judah came to me and said, *"John, sir, I no work now. My wife need me. You have much help. She have no help. I go to help her. Understand?* At that moment, I felt such sadness for him and all I could say was, Yes, I understand. He went to be where he was needed but I really missed his company and still do."

"I have been here for about 15 years now and I figure Judah to be at least 75 years old. I wish that I was in as good a condition as he is, "Doc said wistfully.

John looked at Doc in total disbelief! "WOW, Judah worked with a lot of younger men when he was with me last year and he worked harder than every one of them." After having said that, John walked over to a chair and sat down, all the while still shaking his head in disbelief.

The room became quiet for a few moments when Lisa suddenly spoke up and asked, "Could someone show me the outside area where Cutie Pie will be staying?"

Larry was the first to answer, "Sure come right this way" and he was quickly at the door to the yard. As he opened the door for Lisa and Cutie Pie, he took a deep breath. He had listened to every word spoken so intently that he almost forgot to breathe.

Cutie Pie, now outside and free to run around the enclosure, looked almost comical. Not knowing which way to run first, she just kept running in circles. As if that were not funny enough, then as everyone began coming into the enclosure, she would run up to each one and look at them as if to say, *"Come on. Come on. Run with me. We are free. Free at last."* Each time laughter would begin all over again.

"I have to be on my way to pick up Momma Big-Toe. Hopefully we will see you all later," John said as he walked to the gate.

"OK. OK. Everyone back to work," Doc barked and his staff stumbled over each other as they headed for the door.

"What about Cutie Pie? I should be getting back to school," Lisa said with concern in her voice.

Jane came to her rescue again. "Lisa see that camera on the wall by the door? We can see her. Over there, what looks like a doghouse, is for her to use as a place to go when she wants *"to be alone.'* Lisa had to laugh at Jane's, Ingrid Bergman's, terrible impersonation.

"Thanks. I feel better knowing all of that. I'll check my bus schedule and be on my way."

Lisa glanced at her watch and then at the bus schedule. The time was 11:30 and the next bus was not due until 2 o'clock. "I should have waited inside where it is cooler", she thought just as a loud horn sounded. She almost jumped out of her skin.

It was John. He was about to drive away when he spotted Lisa leaving the animal hospital building. He quickly jerked the truck around, driving in a circle and pulled up next to her.

Lisa looked up at him with blazing blue eyes and said, "Do you have to blow that horn so-o loudly. I almost had a heart attack!"

Sheepishly John responded, "Sorry. I wanted to get your attention."

"Well, you certainly accomplished that!", she said in her best offended voice.

John, stumbling over his next words said, "Momma pick up Big-Toe, No. I mean would you like a lift to the school before I pick up Momma With Big-Toe?

Lisa, at this point smiled at his discomfort saying," I have so much to do before school starts in 2 weeks. That would be great. Thanks" and walked to the passenger side of the truck and climbed in. The silence in the truck was so thick that one could have cut it with a knife.

Then, they both began to speak at the same time which caused them to laugh and thankfully the awkward silence was ended.

Lisa recovered first and asked," How did Momma With Big Toe get her name?"

John smiled and answered, "In their village there are 2 grandmotherly-type women. To be called Momma is a sign of respect for their age, the lives they have lived and their knowledge. Both women are widows, have no living children and no relatives. This village, like other villages, look out for them. When this Momma's toe swelled up 2 weeks ago, she began to be called, Momma With Big-Toe. That made it easier to differentiate between the two Mommas." Grinning from ear-to-ear John continued by saying," I don't know what she will be called when and if her toe is taken care of."

Lisa, caught off guard by his statement, started laughing and responded by saying," Maybe she will be called Momma Who Had Big-Toe or Momma's Big-Toe Gone Now or Momma No Have Big-Toe." At this point tears were running down both John's and Lisa's cheeks.

The school was in sight and another awkward silence started. John, looking at Lisa, said softly, "I really enjoy your company. Especially when your blue eyes aren't blazing."

"What do you mean about my blazing blue eyes?" Hearing that said, John's hair on the back of his neck stood up and he knew that he was on her wrong side again!

Lisa gave him a look and stiffly said, "Thanks for the lift. I hope I did not inconvenience you in any way. Give my regards to Momma With Big-Toe." She then proceeded to climb down from the truck and slammed the door so hard that the trucks' windows rattled.

John sped away as fast as he could, leaving a sand storm in his wake. "Oh, why do I try to be nice to that woman. I can never seem to do or say the right thing at any given moment when I am near her. She intrigues me. I have so many questions I would like her to answer. But now I am thinking why bother." Taking deep breathes he finally calmed down and soon arrived at Momma With Big-Toe's hut.

Lisa, meanwhile almost sprinted into the teachers living quarters. Luckily the caretakers, M and M, were cleaning the kitchen at the back of the first floor. They were loudly singing to one of the new tapes Lisa had given them as a "treat". This gave Lisa hope that they would not hear her as she silently climbed the stairs to her rooms. She did not want to see anyone much less talk to anyone. Her door had a nasty squeak but she anticipated the noise and cautiously opened it.

Lisa was upset and did not know why. Her mind was spinning and her thoughts came like speeding bullets. "This has got to stop. Get control of yourself. You are acting strange and even worse, saying things as if you have no filters in place!" Then speaking out loud to herself, "What is the matter with you? "and as soon as those words left her lips the tears started.

She flipped off her shoes, pulled back the coverlet from her bed, slid into bed and hugged her pillow. "OH! Why do I say such awful things and act no nasty, that's not me? It always seems to be directed at John. Something has to be done and evidently done by me."

Lisa now had a "quest". The word quest was becoming more and more a regular part of her vocabulary, having used it at least once a day in the last three days.

# Chapter 9

*M*eanwhile, John was at Momma's village. As he drove up to her front yard and before he could get out of his truck, she appeared. Momma was colorfully dressed, with a different matching headdress and purse. As always, her wonderful grin and sparkling eyes showed on her soft round face.

*"John, sir you right on time. What is right word for dat? Puntal?",* **she asked as she smiled at him, with a glint in her eyes.**

"That's right. Punctual is what I am known for, especially if it means breakfast, lunch or dinner," he answered with a chuckle.

"You look very stylish, Momma. Do you have big plans for today?" John then asked.

*"When a hansum young man come take me for ride in his truck, I no make him feel bad because of way I dress. I dress special. And remember I see Doc Williams for toe look. He good looker, too,"* she answered in a serious tone.

They rode for a while in silence, when Momma asked John, *"Hokay! What you gonna do about Missy Lisa?"*

John, taken by surprise at her question and his face slowly turning beet red, said, "Ah-h, what do mean, what am I going to do about Missy Lisa"

*"Well, when you two in same place, I see special light spark 'round 'boat of you. You no feel noting?",* Momma quietly asked.

"Oh, Momma. I don't know what is wrong. It seems that we are always at odds", he replied in a frustrating manner.

*"What is odds? Nutin wrong wid two of yous. Powerful feelings make people act funny. Momma know 'bout these tings. You smart man. You will know what to do," a*nd having said that, she closed her eyes and proceeded to take a nap.

John was still taken back by her question. "Well, I am a logical thinker and I will come up with a logical answer. Every question has an answer or a solution or at least that's what I have been repeatedly told," he said softly to himself.

The Bushman Clinic was not far from the Preserve's Animal hospital. John drove to the main entrance and climbed out of the truck to help Momma. She had awakened and was ready for him.

*"You good driver and delivery man. I would not walk dis far. Foot hurts. Tanks for your help.'"* She was soon on her way to the main door when John shouted, "I'll be back to check on you and take you home." Momma waived her arm, acknowledging that she had heard him.

Just then John's walkie talkie beeped and he answered it. John was smiling when the conversation ended and he quickly started to walk to the animal hospital. He knew the ins and outs of both buildings. Maintaining all the buildings on the preserve was his responsibility. Both hospital staffs would agree that he was on top of what had to be taken care of and they were extremely pleased with him as manager.

He found Doc sitting in his office with a stack of papers in front of him. Seeing John, he cried out, "What is going on? What do you want?"

John could tell that Doc was irritated about something. "I'll come back later and maybe you will be in a better mood," John quickly answered.

"Don't be silly. I'm hungry and Maisie has been away picking up supplies. I can't be bothered preparing anything to eat. She will be back soon. She knows that if she finds me passed out cold on the floor, it's because I am malnourished," Doc said and then they both started to laugh.

"Doc, I had a call from the sergeant who is handling the stolen animals case. It seems the court case will be coming up in a few days and he has had no luck in finding any relatives or friends of the boy's family. Do you need help with the animals or mopping the floors? Anything that he could do? I was hoping that there would be a place for him around here and he could room with Larry, Moe and Curley. Oops! I mean just Larry and Moe in the dormitory. I am sure the school will help him. Then there is Momma. Once she knows about him rescuing Cutie Pie, she will be all over him. Maybe like a Granny," and John, gasping for air, finally stopped talking,

"John! I have never heard so-o-o many sentences or thoughts come from you so-o-o fast and in such a short period of time, the entire time I have known you," Doc said in amazement. "You have really given this a lot of thought but what about what the boy wants? Maybe you should go and see him."

"Doc, you are so-o-o right. I'll call the sergeant now and hopefully, arrangements can be made to see the boy this afternoon. For one thing, I would like to know his name and age. See you when I get back," and out to his truck he went, all the while talking on his walkie talkie.

The forty-minute ride seemed as if it would never end. John was so nervous. Memories came flooding back from his childhood. He was 15 when his parents were killed in a car crash. He had never felt so alone. His parents were the story book picture of the perfect couple, the perfect parents and with John they made the perfect family. And they had been.

His Granny came to his rescue. She sold her house, furniture and most of her possessions. She packed up her personal things, some pictures and photo albums and moved into John's home. Granny felt that he needed some continuity in his life and staying in his familiar home and familiar school was the best thing for him. She saw to it that he studied hard and participated in school activities and sports that interested him.

After high school, John choose to commute to the local college. After graduating he found "the" perfect job. Someone or something was watching over him. It was close to home and just like in his college days he wanted to be there for Granny as she aged. Granny had been everything a Granny should be. Wise beyond her years, full of unconditional love, firm when necessary but liked a good joke and what she called "foolishness."

She was an excellent cook and he would watch her as she prepared their meals. Eventually he started writing her recipes in a small notebook. John took over cooking for them when it became too much for Granny. Each time he prepared one of her recipes she would smile and rave over his efforts but also made corrections or suggestions when needed.

John's favorite mental picture of his Granny was of her sitting in her rocking chair. Her hands were always busy with needlework of some kind. When she was crocheting, the faster the needle flew, the faster the rocker rocked and her crossed leg would be swinging even faster. He often thought that the rocking chair would just take off flying sometime to somewhere.

Then three years ago, she quietly passed away in her sleep. Once again, he felt so alone. He was advised to wait a year before making any drastic decisions as to his future. His extended family and friends knew that he wanted to travel, perhaps even work in a foreign country. Animals had been and were still a big part of his life.

His parents and then Granny never minded when he brought home a stray cat or dog. John understood that the animal could only stay until a good home was found for it. Part-time jobs with his neighborhood veterinarian, during high school and college, furthered his love for all creatures.

## Chapter 10

The police outpost was coming into view and John could hardly sit still while driving onto the driveway. The truck screeched to a halt and he was out of the truck as soon as he turned the engine off.

Walking to the building's front door, he mumbled to himself, "Oh, good. In this afternoon heat, no one is around to hear that screech and I hope no one inside the building heard it either. After all, this is a police outpost!"

Sergeant Kane was sitting at his desk when John entered his office. "So good to put a face to a name," the Sergeant said. Then he smiled as he stood up and extended his hand in greeting.

Grasping the sergeant's hand, John said, "Yes sir, I agree. Thanks for setting up this meeting so quickly. I appreciate your help and now, where do we go for me to meet… Oh! Surely the boy has a name?" John was hoping that he was not appearing to be as nervous as he was feeling.

"Yes, he has a name. It is Matt Thompson. As to your thanking me, I am hoping that you can do something for him. He is such a nice boy. I would hate to see him go to prison. Here is what we know about him. His Mom and Dad were missionaries from the US and Matt was born here. It seems that he and his family were trying to flee from an attack on their village when his Mom and Dad were killed. Matt lay down and pretended to have been killed. He waited for hours before making any kind of movement. As soon as it started to get dark he ran away from the village, afraid that the killers would return.

After a while, he saw the caravan with the men and the animals. Some animals were tied to the back of a rickety old cart. Others were in cages that had been placed in larger carts. He didn't know that the animals were stolen. He tagged along, making himself useful. The thieves just accepted him as another lost boy needing food and protection. Imagine, all those bad guys speaking so very highly of him and giving him such good references. It was as if Matt was applying for a job. Well, anyway, I had him brought here from the station up north to save you some travel time. Let's go and see him now. I won't say any more, 'cause that way you'll get any info' straight from the horse's mouth." Grinning from ear to ear, Sergeant Kane then took some keys from a series of hooks on his office wall and pointed to his office door.

The two men walked down a long hallway that held mostly empty cells. The occupied cells contained sleeping occupants. Then John saw Matt and his heart plummeted. "He must be about the same age I was when my parents died," he thought. John quickly glanced down at Matt's paperwork and saw the line marked AGE:14 years.

Sergeant Kane unlocked and then opened the cell door, saying," Matt, this is John the gentleman I spoke about and he would like to visit. Is that all right?

"Yes sir, I have been hoping for some company. Pretty quiet and lonely here," Matt answered.

"Sergeant, is there somewhere else that Matt and I can go and talk, "John asked while giving the sergeant a wide-eyed look. Sergeant Kane got the message and said, "Come along Matt and I'll find somewhere more comfortable for the two of you."

The three of them walked a short way down another hall and entered a room slightly larger than Matt's holding cell. But the room had a ceiling fan! It was doing a good job of moving the air and making the room feel cooler. The holding cell had been stuffy and not well ventilated. This room had a table and two chairs. Sergeant Kane thoughtfully placed two chilled water bottles on the table and left the room.

"Matt the reason I am here is to ask you some questions," John said as he opened his water bottle. He pointed to Matt and then to the other bottle, smiled and said, "Drink up. Hydrate is the mantra for this country."

"You're English is very good and you don't seem to be a native. Tell me about yourself.", John asked between sips.

Matt smiled and answered, "Yes, sir. My English comes from my English, speaking parents… and suddenly a sense of sadness came over him. He composed himself and started again. "My English comes from my English, speaking parents and the mission school. My grandparents started the school some umpteen million years ago and when they retired, my parents came to run the school. I was born here." Matt sat still and a tear slid down his cheek. John could only surmise that Matt was remembering that horrible scene at his village.

John began speaking softly about the baby camel. He told Matt what had transpired since he had last seen it. John was hoping to bring Matt back to a better mental place. Then when John got to the part about Lisa naming the camel, Cutie Pie, Matt had just taken a gulp of water and almost choked. He began laughing and John took this as a good sign.

"Matt, your care and concern about Cutie Pie... and at this point they both started laughing. John tried to continue but had to take another minute or two to compose himself.

"OK. Let me let me try this again. Matt, your actions in getting and John was very careful to say, the baby camel, to safety and out of harm's way, has impressed and endeared you to everyone who has heard the story. These folks want to help you. In fact, it was Sergeant Kane who fist spoke about the injustice that would happen if you were sent to jail or prison. That is what got me, I mean all of us interested in your situation. Here is what we suggest but it will be you who makes the final decision."

John outlined the proposal in a business-like way, but also in a caring way. Basically, it boiled down to Matt living on the preserve, bunking in the dormitory, attending the mission school and helping at the animal hospital.

Matt listened intently to each detail. His eyes grew brighter and his smile even larger with each suggestion.

"I can't believe so many folks want to help me. I am humbled by their kind intentions and would be foolish to not take them up on those suggestions. So, my answer is," *yes,* sir."

Standing up and stretching his long body, John said, "Well, let's go find the sergeant, sign some papers and head back to the preserve."

"Yes, sir. I am ready," and Matt picked up his small bundle of neatly folded clothes consisting of a tee shirt, underwear and a pair of cut-off jeans. Sitting beside the bundle was a pair of used sandals.

"Sergeant Kane's wife sent all of this to me. Great people and even their son came for a visit."

As they walked down the hallway, John's thoughts were concentrating on the next step. It would be a big step for him. What he had not told Matt was that he would have to agree to be Matt's probation officer for the next 12 months. The judge had agreed to Probation Before Sentencing to correct a possible miscarriage of justice.

Sergeant Kane was back at his desk and saw them through the large office window. He arose from his chair and went to the door to greet them.

"I guess your answer was, "*yes*", Matt since you have your belongings with you," he said and smiled at Matt.

"Now let me explain how this works. The judge has appointed John to be, well, like an extended family member to you. John has agreed to do this and he will be reporting your behavior to the judge every month for the next 12 months. At the end of the 12 months if you have behaved yourself, then the judge will make this legal stuff go away. This is, in and of itself, a big responsibility for you and especially John. Do you understand any or all of this, Matt?"

Matt had been staring at the sergeant with wide eyes. When hearing what John was willing to do for him, his eyes grew even larger. He quickly looked at John and said, "Sir, you would do all of that for me? I don't know what to say, except "Thank you."

John was pleased with Matt's sincere "Thank you." Taking up a pen, he signed the paperwork which of course was in triplicate.

"Let's get on the road and get some food. I am starving," John said as he winked at Sergeant Kane.

All three shook hands and said their good-byes. Matt looked at the sergeant, walked over to him and gave him a big hug. He then turned around and followed John outside.

## Chapter 11

*A*s they rode along, Matt sat quietly trying to take in everything that had just happened. John, meanwhile was mentally planning the rest of his day. First, drop off Matt at the preserve animal hospital. Second, check on Momma. Third, see about something to eat. Maybe dinner with Doc, Maisie, Matt and Larry, Moe and Curley, too. He was hungry before these thoughts. Now thinking about Maisie's cooking, he became hungrier and his stomach started to growl.

"Matt, my plans are to stop at the animal hospital. Hopefully we can have dinner at Doc's commissary. That's what I call his kitchen when it is around any mealtime. There are no fast food joints here, so we take advantage of each-others hospitality," and John chuckled when he said it.

"What's a fast food joint," Matt asked quizzically.

John was taken back for a moment and then realized that Matt had never been to a large metropolitan city.

"It is a place for ordering food that is quickly prepared for you. Some have tables for you to sit down and eat. If you carry the food out to eat somewhere else. That is called "carry-out". Whew! I hope my explanation answers his question.

Matt smiled and said," It all sounds like fun and I am hungry, too."

The afternoon sun was high in the sky and the air was heating. Up. They pulled up to the hospital steps, jumped from the truck and ran inside.

"Wow, this is some layout," Matt exclaimed as his eyes took in his surroundings.

"Oh, great! Doc and the staff are not here. That means they must be having dinner. Let's go get something to eat," John quickly said and pointed to the back door. Matt didn't hesitate and was out the door with John following close behind.

Matt suddenly stopped in his tracks, causing John to almost walk into him. "I have no idea where to go. Lead the way and I will follow you," Matt said laughing.

John took the lead and soon they were climbing the steps to Doc's house. The aroma of something delicious filled their noses. It was easy to follow the smells and the hearty conversations coming from the back of the house. When they entered the dining room, silence descended like a theater curtain at the end of a show.

Doc spoke first. "Well, we have to remember to lock the doors because one never does know who or what could come in." Everyone started to laugh and Doc stood up and pointed to two chairs.

"Come on and join us. We just started to eat all these leftovers, so you better grab something before it's all gone."

John and Matt quickly sat down and began filling their plates. Momma With Big-Toe was sitting next to Doc and smiled at the newcomers. Everyone continued eating and John, after eating a few mouthfuls, said," Listen up everyone. Let me introduce Matt Thompson. He is the hero who saved Cutie Pie," and laughter started as soon as he said the camel's name. John just rolled his eyes and continued with the introductions.

Surprisingly, Momma With Big-Toe had remained quiet but now that there was a pause in the conversations, she took advantage of it.

*"John, sir! Doc Williams look at me toe and he tell me, me toe was stubbed. He tell me what to do and he finish with me. He call Doc to find you. No find you and he bring me here to eat and wait for you. Then Doc take me to see baby camel and she doin' good. She remember me,"* and after saying that, Momma's toothless smile almost covered her entire face.

*"Thank you, Doc and thank you Maisie for the food. You say these foods are leftovers. What be leftovers?"*

At this point, everyone tried very hard not to laugh at her serious tone and her quizzical look as she asked the question. Maisie smiled and answered her, "This is what was not eaten at dinner the night before or nights before. I save everything for another night."

Momma grinned, saying, *"I understand. You good worker. No waste food."*

Jane, Joe and Larry, as if on cue, got up from their chairs, cleared the dishes from the table and took them to the kitchen. They returned carrying desserts, plates, more paper napkins and plastic forks.

John groaned and looked at Maisie. "I have to stop coming here and eating. It's bad for my health. I think I might explode if I eat anther thing. But I will take a doggy bag for later if that's OK."

Momma and Matt looked at John and Matt was the first to say, "What is a doggy bag?"

Once again Maisie took the lead and answered," When you cannot eat all your food at a meal, you can ask to take it with you. It is then placed in something like a bag or a dish and you take it with you."

*"Oh, I save food tings for baby camel in a sack. Now I know say," doggy bag,"* Momma said smiling but with a serious look.

John had been watching Momma. She was glowing and enjoying every second of being there. He really did not want to tell her that it was time to go but finally said to her, "Momma, let's get ready and head back to the village." Then looking at Matt, he said, "Larry or Moe will show you your new digs and the rest of the place. Oh, and then take you to see Cutie Pie, too." Hearing himself say that, he laughed all the way to his truck.

Momma was soon settled in his truck when he noticed for the first time the bright red bow on her big toe. "Momma, what a pretty red bow you have on your toe!", he exclaimed.

Momma sat up and beamed. *"Yes, Doc Williams say that my toe need special bow and nurse tie it on me toe for me. Now everyone in village see my important big toe because it soon be gone. I be sad when toe not big 'cause my name not be true,"* and a sad look appeared on her face.

John quickly said," But Momma, you can always keep Momma With Big-Toe as your name. Then when anyone asks you about your name, you will have quite a story to tell."

When hearing John say that, Momma smiled her brightest toothless smile and said*," John, sir. You, smart man."* Their ride was almost over when Momma looked at John and quietly said*," John, sir. There be more to Missy Lisa and her name for baby camel. Name Cutie Pie important to her. You help her. She need good friend."*

They arrived at Momma's hut and John helped her from the truck. She tightly held on to his arm, all the while studying his face. Looking directly into his eyes she asked, *"You hear what Momma say? John, sir?"*

"Yes, Momma. I hear you and I will try to be her friend," John answered. "You have the instructions from Doc Williams so now go and take care of your toe."

*"Yes, I will and tanks to you for so good a day, John, sir",* and Momma turned around, starting to walk towards her hut. But for some reason she turned around again to wave goodbye. What she saw was John walking with his head bent down and his shoulders sagging, showing her a tired but thoughtful man.

Momma softly said to herself, "He *tinking 'bout Missy Lisa. John, sir you know what to do."* She turned around once again and walking to her front door entered her hut.

Driving away, John felt like he had a heavy weight on his shoulders. "Momma is right, you need to do something. Maybe having a new start with Lisa would help. We really did well the first time we met. Yeah, but would she agree? Well, dah, you won't know unless you ask," and he turned the truck around and headed for home.

## Chapter 12

*L*isa had been very busy the last two days. With school to start soon, she had the classrooms to set up, lessons to prepare and more books to unpack. The afternoon heat was taking its toll. "Whew! I need a break. Hydrate. Hydrate, the mantra of Africa. If I drink anymore, I will gurgle when I walk," and she headed for the fridge all the while laughing at the mental picture that had been created in her mind.

With the cold, water bottle in hand, Lisa walked out the door to the front porch. She flipped the ceiling fan switch to on and plopped down on the well-worn lounge chair. She was just about to doze off when in the distance she saw a truck coming her way. "Who can this be? I'm not expecting any more school supplies or visitors," she thought to herself and just then she recognized John's truck.

"Oh, no! Something must be wrong. But with who? Cutie Pie? That's who it must be," and rising from her chair she jumped from the porch and ran to meet John. As soon as the truck came to a stop, Lisa was beside the truck's driver side door.

"What's wrong? Why are you here?" she asked.

John quickly opened the door, jumped out and softly said, "Calm down. Nothing is wrong. Everyone is fine, including Cutie Pie. I just came to talk to you and bring you up to date. Let's get out of this heat. Would the porch be cool enough?", he asked.

"Yes, there's a ceiling fan. Come along and I will get you something cold to drink," Lisa answered and she began briskly walking ahead of John as they headed for the porch.

John sat down in one of the two chairs to wait for Lisa. She quickly returned with his water and some cookies on a plate and sat in the other chair. For some reason, she stopped herself from saying, "You are sitting in my chair." She knew deep down inside of herself that her reactions to his words or actions, had to change.

After finishing most of his water bottle, John smiled and said," What would we do without refrigeration and of all things, I have given myself an ice cream headache!" They both started to laugh.

Lisa still laughing, replied, "I haven't heard that expression in a long time. Maybe even as far back as my childhood." Then John saw a dullness cover her eyes. He kept himself from saying anything, hoping to give her time to compose herself.

"John, I am so sorry for the way I have been acting. The baby camel brought back sad memories from my childhood." At this point, John raised his hand trying to stop her and he started to say," Lisa you don't have to…" when she interrupted him and said, "Yes, John.

I do need to explain the *whys* and *what fors*, of my actions." Having said that, Lisa started telling her story.

"My Dad was a veterinarian. He had a small practice near a medium sized city, Pondsville, in Washington state. The circus was coming to Pondsville and as they passed our property, a mother camel gave birth to a female calf. The circus hands knew immediately that something was wrong with the baby camel. My Dad's practice was closer than the Pondsville vet's clinic and they brought the baby camel to my Dad.

Our house was part of the building that held his clinic and office. I had been doing homework at the kitchen table when my Dad called for me to come help. It was Friday evening and none of his staff was around. As soon as I saw how tiny and fragile the baby camel looked, I called out, "Oh, what a Cutie Pie," and the name stuck the entire time the camel was with us."

Lisa stopped talking and looked off into the distance as if seeking help, from someone, somewhere, with the words to help her finish her story. "Dad examined Cutie Pie and then taking me aside said," Lisa, do what you can to make her comfortable. She will not be with us long." I looked at him and answered," Yes, Dad, I understand what you are saying to me".

"You see, my Mom had died the year before. Our doctor had come for Mom's weekly checkup and when the examination was over, Doc Sorensen and Dad went for a walk. It was during that walk when my Dad was informed of her condition and prognosis. When they returned, Doc Sorensen left and Dad called me into his office.

"Lisa, do what you can to make your Mom comfortable. She will not be with us for long. Those were the exact same words that he had said to me about the baby camel. I made it my job to stay with Cutie Pie every minute of those two days she was with us. Cutie Pie passed away sleeping in my arms. I felt so helpless again, just as I had when my Mom passed. Then two years ago my Dad passed away. I think it is so hard to be left behind and to let them go. I was told so many times that, *"time heals all things,"* but it doesn't say how long that *"time"* will be. Last year I decided to sell everything and *"to go and do some good, somewhere."* That is why I am here in Africa teaching at the mission school."

"Well, now you have heard my story", Lisa said, while smiling sadly.

"You have been through a lot and I admire your tenacity. As far as *"doing some good",* you have only been here a short time, but you surely must know how much you are liked and how much your work is appreciated."

Hoping to help lighten her mood, John said, "Now let me bring you up to date on today's happenings," and he proceeded to tell about Momma With Big-Toe's visit to the hospital, arrangements he made with Sergeant Kane to help Matt and then finishing with the dinner at Doc and Maisie's home.

At the mention of Matt's name, Lisa sat up straight, waiting for him to finish speaking.

'"You agreed to help Matt by being a kind of sponsor or parole officer for him. Oh, what a wonderful thing for you to do." Lisa said and then asked, "Can I help in some way?"

"Thanks. That would be great. He will need to be accepted into the mission school and that is one way you can help. While listening to your *"story"* it reminded me somewhat of my growing up years and why I am here", and John proceeded to tell his story.

The late afternoon sun was now much lower in the sky. For some time, Lisa and John had just been sitting silently on the porch, lost in their own thoughts but it was a comfortable silence. John felt that something had happened between them, something good.

He was sure that they both knew that any time spent together from this point on would be different and he was sure that they were both looking forward to it.

CPSIA information can be obtained
at www.ICGtesting.com
Printed in the USA
FSOW03n2050281017
40416FS

9 781545 617243